Dairy Farmers

Elsie Nelley

Dairy farmers are people
who live and work on farms.

Many dairy farmers own the farms.
Some have lived on their farms for a long time.

Dairy farmers have to work very hard
because they keep herds of cows for their milk.

Each morning, dairy farmers get up very early.

Some farmers ride their farm bikes
to the fields where the cows are kept.
They bring the cows to the milking shed
so they can be milked.

Sometimes, the same cow leads the herd
to the milking shed.

Dairy farmers care about their cows.
They even give them names.

Dairy farmers milk their cows with machines.
They milk them in the morning
and again in the afternoon.

Lots of cows can be milked at the same time.
Before the machines are put on the cows,
the farmers wash under the cow's stomach.

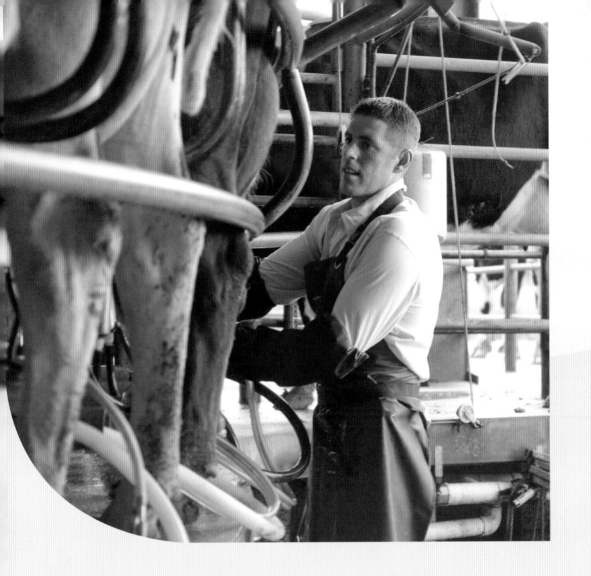

The floor of a milking shed can get very wet.
The farmers walk carefully so they don't slip over.

The milk is kept cold in a tank
until a big truck takes it away to a factory.

After the cows have been milked,
they walk slowly back to a field.

Then, the farmers clean the milking machines
with hot water.
They wash the floors and the yards outside
with big hoses, too.

Everything in the milking sheds
must be kept very clean.

Dairy farmers have many jobs to do every day.
Fences have to be checked and fixed,
and ditches have to be dug.

In spring, there are calves to care for.
In summer, farmers let the grass
on their farms grow long.
They cut it to make hay.
They feed this hay to their animals in winter.

Farmers move heavy loads from one place to another with their tractors.

When dairy farmers work outside,
they always wear big boots.

In summer, they put on sunhats and sunscreen.
In winter, they wear warm hats and thick jackets
because it gets cold out in the fields.

Dairy farmers work inside, too.
They check their computers each day,
to find out how much milk
has gone to the factory.

They can send emails and pay their bills.
They can buy things online from shops in the city.

Dairy farmers give their cows
grass or hay to eat
and clean water to drink.

A vet will come to the farm to help cows that are sick.

Dairy farmers always want their cows to be healthy.

Dairy farmers work very hard every day. The milk from their cows helps people to stay healthy.

Children who drink a lot of milk grow strong bones.